CW01218963

For David Birks and David Knowles, who have taught
me beautiful lessons about treasuring life and the
natural world around us.
—Lisa M. Hendey

To my daughter Alice
who deeply loves the nature that surrounds her!
—Giuliano Ferri

I Am Earth's Keeper

Written by **LISA M. HENDEY**
Illustrated by **GIULIANO FERRI**

PARACLETE PRESS
BREWSTER, MASSACHUSETTS

I slip from my bed
and grab my favorite oar.
We tiptoe quite silently
out the back door.

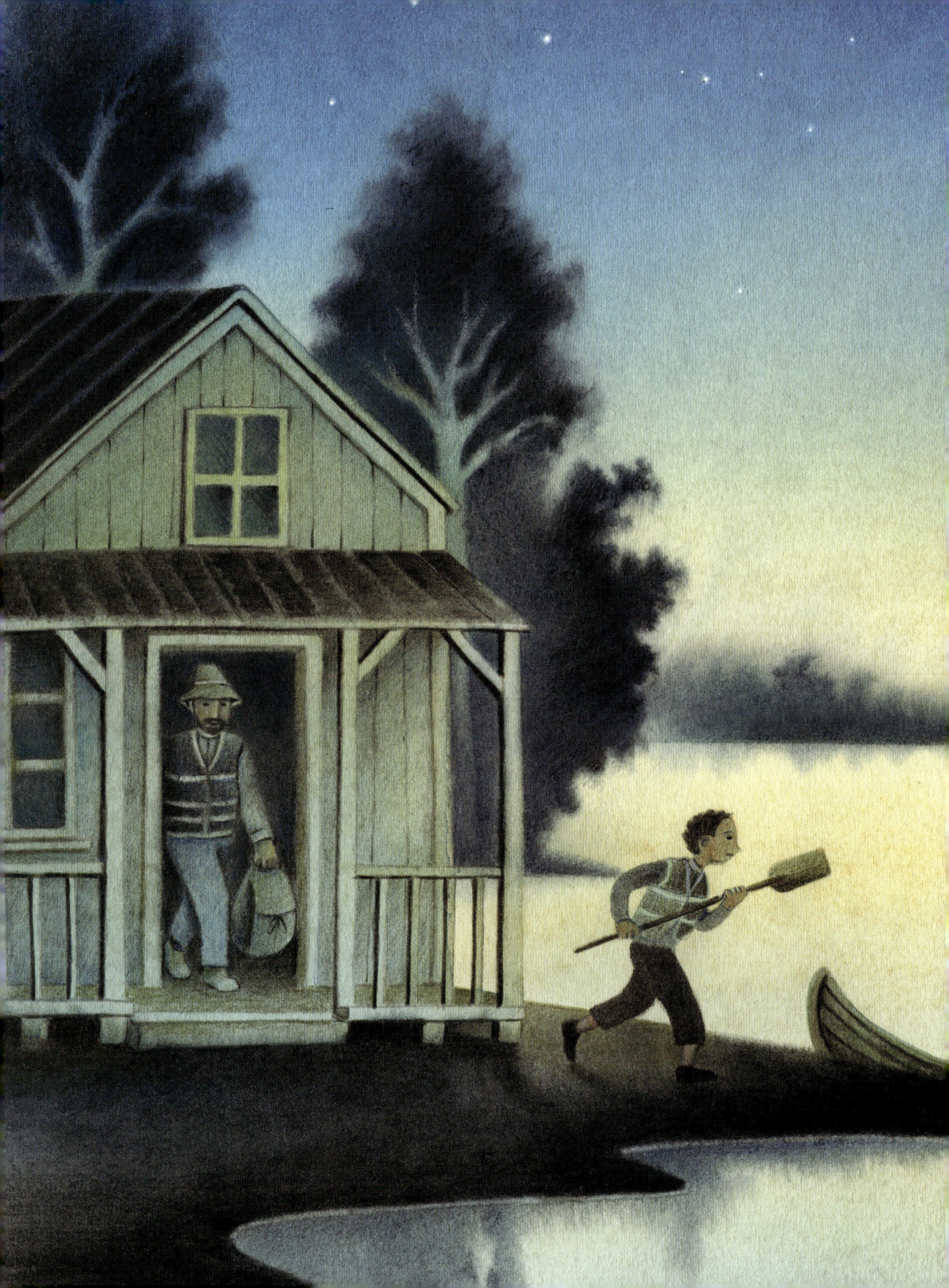

My kayak slides, slippery,
from Mud into Lake.
Great Mother Sun's up
but not fully awake.

We row to the middle,
surveying this Land.
The Frogs swim beside us,
a hidden jazz band.

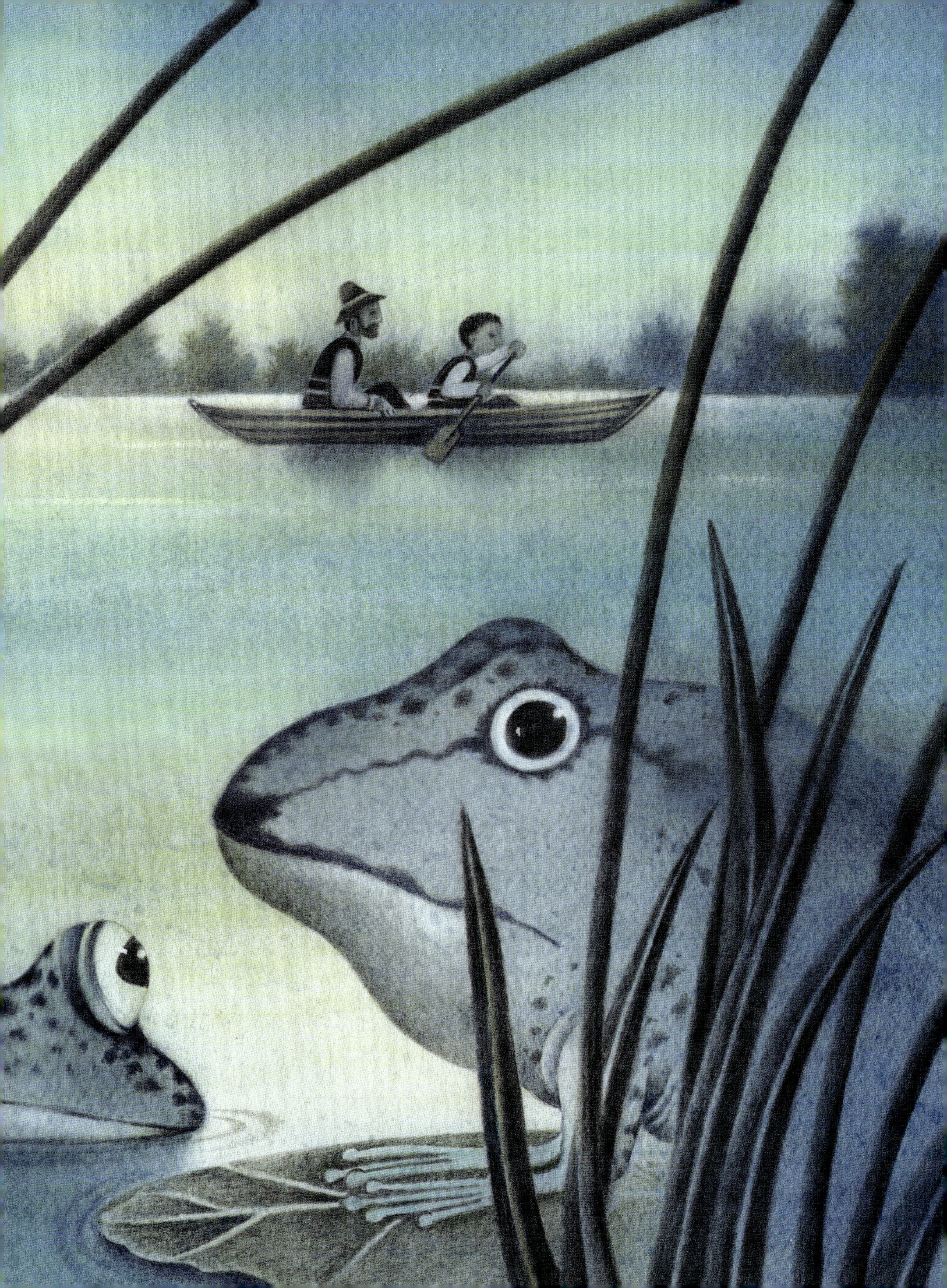

Sun slips above Clouds
and everything's changed.
Land and Sky flip
and my view's rearranged.

Sky is up, Water's down,
or so I've been told.
But Clouds are below me.
They're circles of gold.

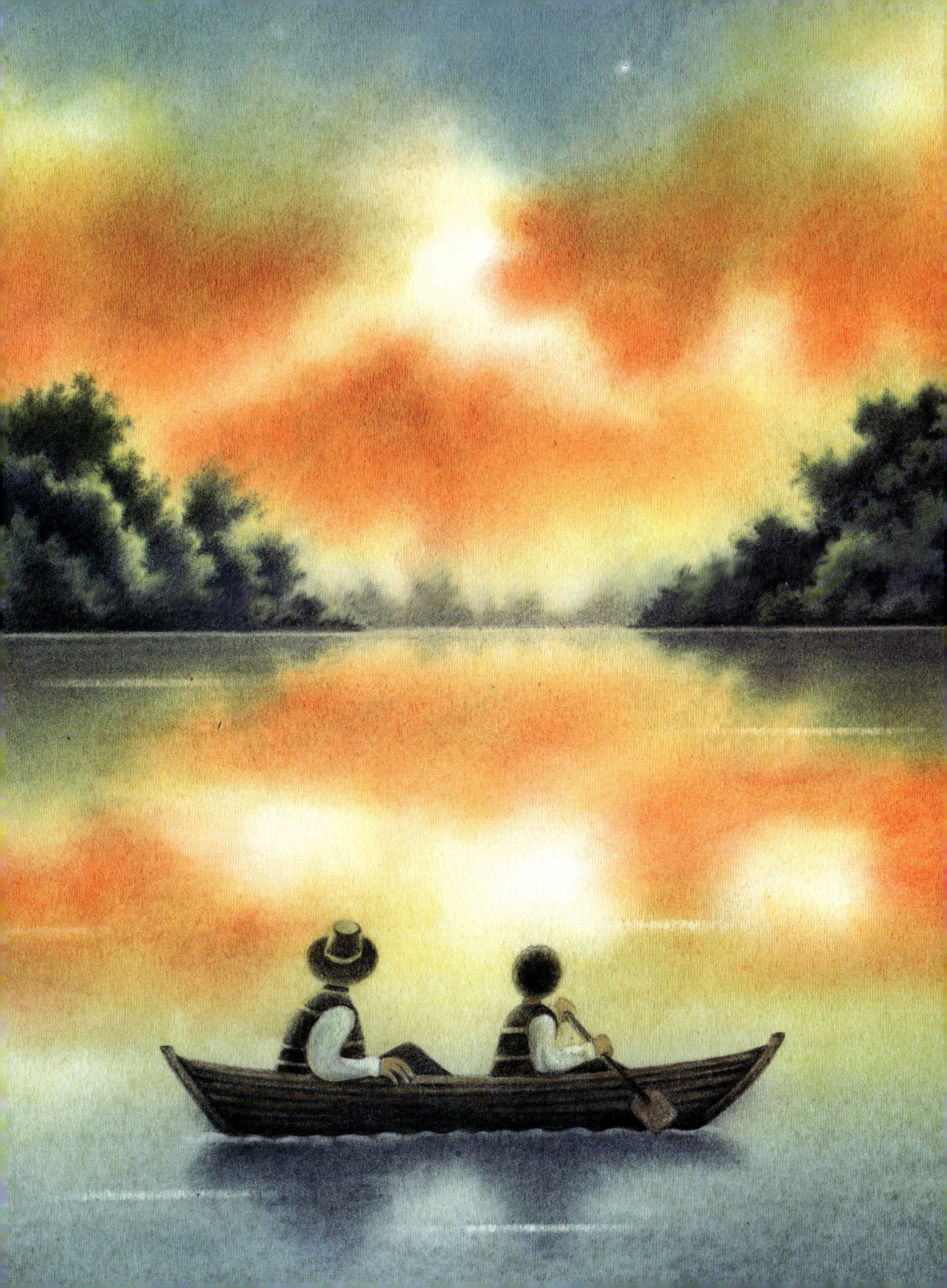

Miss Pond's upside down.
Is Sir Sky here or there?
Can I fly through the Clouds,
chasing Bass, racing Bear?

Horizon's a mirror,
his colors so loud.
I could jump from my boat
and land inside a Cloud.

Will I meet Sister Bird
or greet Brave Brother Fish?
Will I bump into Star
or tell 'Gator my wish?

Today, like Old Beaver,
I'll jump bravely in,
break right through the Clouds,
feel the breeze on my skin.

All glory above me
and glory below.
Is Heaven around me?
Oh, when will I know?

Today, for this moment,
I rest and I think.
I float, looking up,
then I flip but don't sink.

Above me is Hawk,
and below me is Carp.
We all dance together
as Wind plays her harp.

The Clouds paint their picture,
and tell me their tale.
The story repeats
yet will never grow stale.

For ours is a kingdom
that needs love and care.
Belonging together's
a gift that we share.

Each Mammal and Bird,
every River and Stream,
and me as their partner—
we make a great team.

Our mission's to honor
this kingdom of gold,
to treasure and love her,
but loosen our hold.

I climb through the Clouds
back up into my perch.
"It's time you get home now,"
calls old Brother Birch.

"You've had your adventure."
He rustles his leaves.
"Your work now awaits you."
I roll up my sleeves.

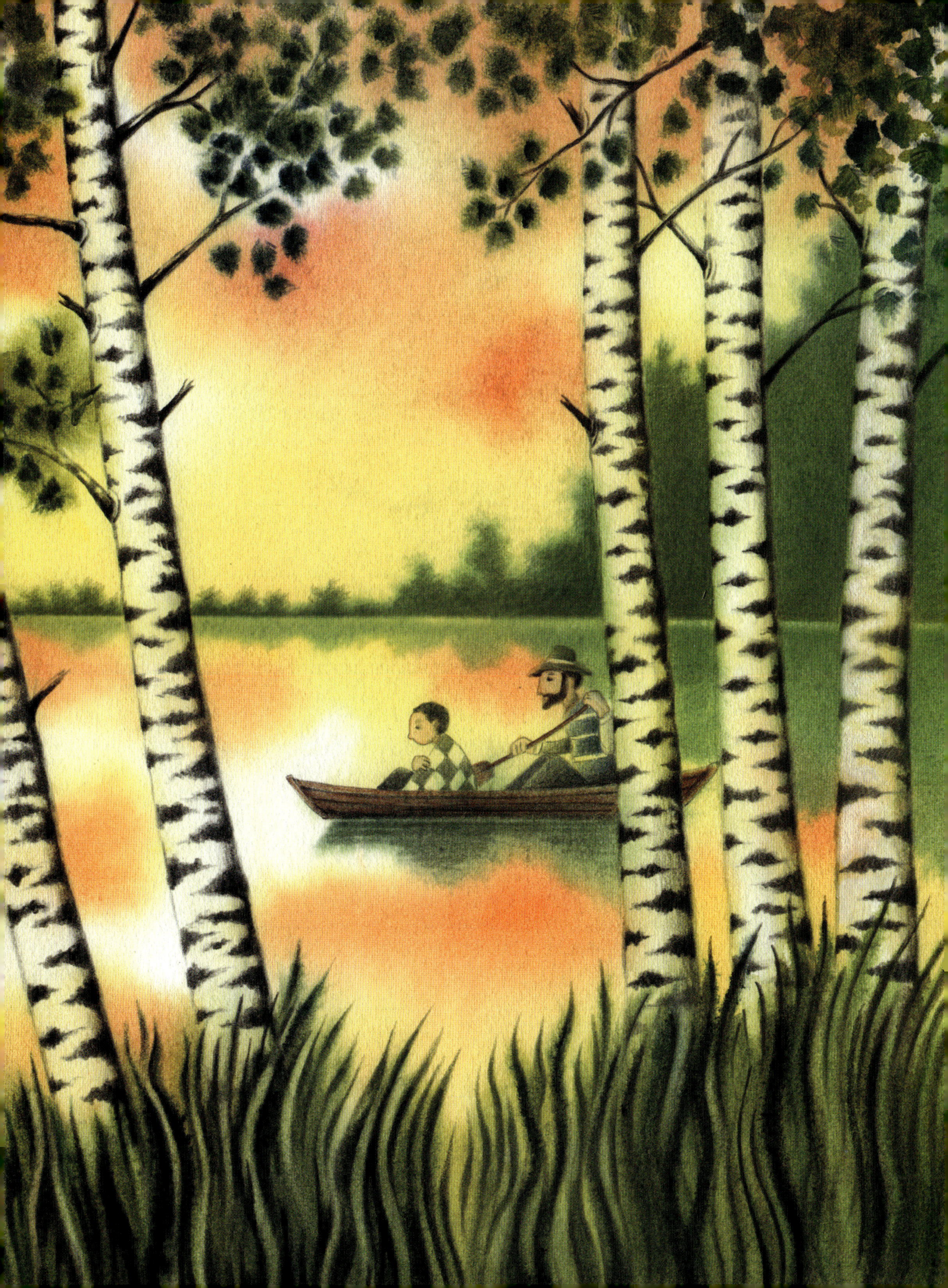

Tomorrow we'll come back.
Then maybe I'll know...
Are answers above me
or somewhere below?

For now, I can't guess,
but each day, I will try.
If I stay in our boat,
I won't learn how to fly.

If I stay in our boat,
I'll miss life's awesome dance.
So I'll paddle and swim,
taking every big chance.

Today when you wake,
you've a promise to keep.
Explore your own kingdom.
Take each giant leap.

Our World is a gift,
one to treasure and share.
We each play a part
every day in her care.

Love her,
Know her.
Protect her.
Grow her.

You might plant a tree,
bike or hike where you go,
and buy less, recycle,
let birds and bees grow.

When we limit our footprint,
we help our Earth thrive.
Let's plant and sustain
so we'll keep her alive.

Each morning, the Artist
sets out to create.
Walk with care.
Love and cherish.

Your journey awaits.

Dear Parents, Teachers, and Caregivers:

The book you hold in your hands was inspired by a photo my friend David took while kayaking on a pond near his home in the pre-dawn hours. When sharing this glorious vista—water and sunrise melded into one majestic work of art—David asked, "Is the sky up or down?" David's image captivated me and inspired me to reflect upon Francis of Assisi's masterpiece, "The Canticle of Brother Sun and Sister Moon."

I hope my words and the lovely images created here by Giuliano Ferri will spark your imagination to connect more deeply with creation and develop an ever-deepening sense of commitment to serving as a "keeper" of our earth.

Lisa

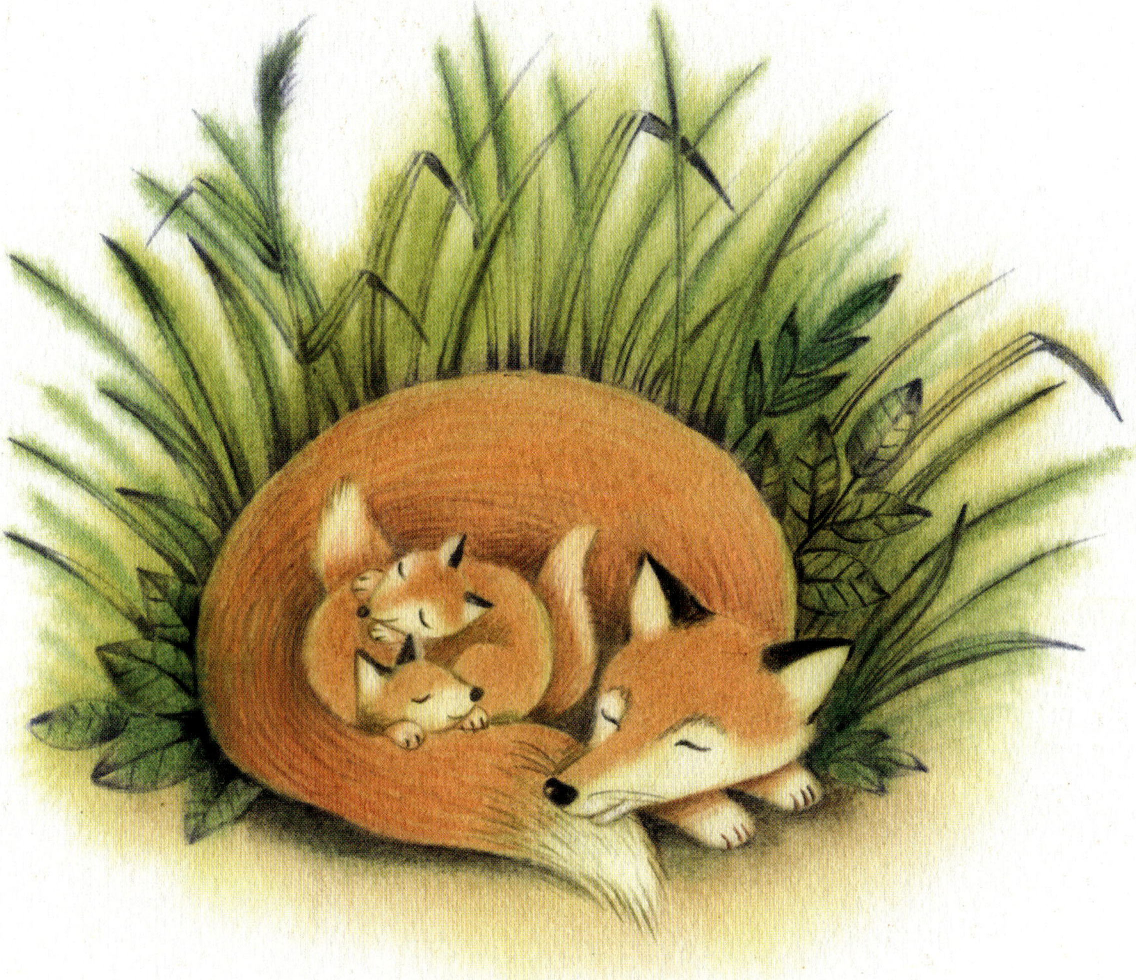